HAPPY TODAY

to my gorgeous boys

ALEX

ADAM

AND

RHYS.

lots and lots and lots

of love

ROS xxx

MUM + DAD CAN READ IT TO!

First edition: May 1999

ISBN: 0-86381-564-2

Scanning and cover design: Smala, Caernarfon; printing: Interprint, Melita.

Published in Wales by Gwasg Carreg Gwalch, 12 Iard yr Orsaf, Llanrwst, Dyffryn Conwy LL26 0EH.
Tel: 01492 642031   Fax: 01492 641502
E-mail: books@carreg-gwalch.co.uk   Internet: www.carreg-gwalch.co.uk

Once Upon a Time in Wales

A book of history and legend
with additional notes and activities

John Owen Huws

translated from Welsh by Siân Lewis

Illustrations:
Gini Wade

Contents

The legends and historical tales

Additional notes and activities

Melangell

Once upon a time in Wales there was a prince called Brochwel. He was the prince of Powys and a very rich man. Brochwel lived at the court of Pengwern, but he was often away from home. He loved to go hunting. For hours and hours he would follow the trail of a fox or a wolf, a stag or a boar. Because he was so rich, he had no need to work. He could hunt every day.

One day Brochwel had decided to hunt far from home. At dawn he and his men got ready to leave the court.

'I'm sure we'll be lucky today, Brochwel,' said one.

'Yes indeed,' said another.
 'There's nothing better than the meat of the red deer.'

'Who knows what we'll catch?' said Brochwel as he hung his golden horn round his neck. 'Off we go!'

The huntsmen galloped away on their fine horses. Two fierce packs of hounds followed close behind.

Brochwel and his men headed for the distant hills. Soon they were galloping down a long valley in a part of Powys that was new to them.

The hounds began to bark. The prince blew his golden horn. A red deer had dashed from the shelter of the trees and the huntsmen gave chase.

The first hounds were already hard on its heels, when the red deer darted away and disappeared.

'Don't worry!' shouted Brochwel. 'We'll soon find another.'

At that moment a grey wolf rushed past the hounds and they all chased after it. But the grey wolf also escaped. So did a wild boar. And so did a red fox.

By this time Brochwel was in a very bad temper. He couldn't go back to Pengwern empty-handed. He had to catch something...

The huntsmen galloped on. The valley got narrower and narrower. Soon it was so narrow, there was no room for an animal to escape.

'A hare!' shouted the prince. 'After it!'

The little grey creature ran for its life with the hounds and the hunters close behind.

'Don't you dare lose this one,' said Brochwel.

9

He blew his horn to urge the hounds on. At last he was in luck. They were reaching the end of the valley and the hare had no hope of escape.

Suddenly a young woman stepped out from beneath the shade of a tree. The hare ran to her and hid beneath her long dress.

'Let that hare go at once!' roared Brochwel.

'And let you kill her? No, I will not,' said the young woman.

'I am Prince Brochwel. No one stands in my way.'

'And I am Melangell. No one is allowed to kill my animals.'

'If you don't move, I'll set the hounds on you,' said Brochwel.

'Do whatever you like. I won't let you touch this little hare.'

'We'll soon see about that,' Brochwel said. He sounded his horn to drive the hounds on. But the hounds would not move. However loud the prince shouted, they remained perfectly still. It was as if they had understood Melangell's words.

'Tell me who you really are,' said the prince.

'I am Melangell, as I told you. I have come here to worship God and to look after the animals of this valley.'

When he heard this, Brochwel fell on his knees.

'You are a saint! I'm sorry I have been so cruel. From now on this valley will be yours. You may do as you like and no one will hunt here.'

At once wild animals of every kind came out of the woods. There were deer, wolves, rabbits, wild boar and many foxes. There were also birds of all kinds. They were no longer afraid. Saint Melangell had saved them.

* * *

The name of the valley where this story took place is Pennant Melangell. The church that Melangell built is still there. The saint became famous for her love of animals. To this day the people of the area have a strange name for hares. I wonder if you can guess what it is. They call them 'Melangell's little lambs', because of the little grey hare that hid beneath Melangell's skirts.

The Secret of Bala Lake

Bala Lake is the biggest natural lake in Wales. Another name for it is Llyn Tegid. It is three and a half miles long and half a mile wide. Many years ago there was no lake. A large town stood in this very place and this is the story of what happened to it.

The town of Bala once stood in a beautiful wooded valley, so the old folk say. Though it was in such a fine spot, it was ruled by a wicked prince. His name was Tegid Foel. Tegid Foel owned all the land in the valley, but he was a very cruel man. He treated people badly. He even killed those whom he did not like.

After a few years the people of the town heard a voice saying:
'Vengeance will come! Vengeance will come!'

No one knew where the voice came from. It seemed to come from the sky.

Tegid Foel heard the voice too. It made no difference to him. He only laughed an evil laugh and behaved more cruelly than ever.

In time the words changed. This is what the people heard:

'Vengeance will come with the children's children! Vengeance will come with the children's children!'

One day Dafydd, the old harpist who lived in the hills, was ordered to go to the palace. He had to play his harp at a feast. Tegid Foel's son had had a baby son and everyone had to celebrate.

The old man remembered the words:

'Vengeance will come with the children's children!'

He was afraid that something would happen at the feast, but he dare not refuse to play his harp. He knew how cruel Tegid Foel could be.

Dafydd felt better when he reached the palace. Everyone was dancing and having such fun that Dafydd soon forgot about Tegid

Foel. His fingers twinkled over the harp strings. The faster he played, the faster the guests danced and the more they laughed.

Suddenly the old harpist heard a small soft voice:

'Vengeance has come.'

Had he really heard those words? He listened carefully and this time there was no doubt.

'Vengeance has come.'

Dafydd had no time to worry about the cruel prince. He had to get away. He even left his harp. He ran out of the palace. He ran out of the town. He ran up to the hills overlooking the valley.

On the hillside Dafydd stopped for breath. Perhaps he had been foolish. It was a fine quiet night. There was no hint of ruin nor revenge. His best plan was to return to the palace. He could be back before the next dance. With luck Tegid Foel wouldn't notice that he had been away.

By this time the mist was rolling down from the mountains. Dafydd was in such a hurry that he missed the path and realised he was lost. Now he was really in trouble. The prince would know he had gone missing and that would be the end of him.

All night the old harpist wandered hopelessly. When dawn broke, he saw the path and hurried downhill towards town. But when he got there, the town had disappeared! A huge lake filled the valley floor. His harp was floating on the still waters. Tegid Foel and his palace had gone for ever. Llyn Tegid had taken their place.

Some say that that the bells of the old town of Bala can still be heard on quiet summer

nights. Some say that once upon a time fishermen would see the ruins of the old town in the water beneath their boats.

Perhaps divers will one day find the town of Tegid Foel. After all there are many strange things beneath the waters of Llyn Tegid. A rare fish, which is called a gwyniad, lives in the lake. They say that a monster lives there too. His name is Tegi, but that's another story...

The Rush Fish of River Conwy

The weather in Wales had been very poor. In early winter it rained heavily and the rivers burst their banks. Then came a heavy blanket of snow over all the land. Spring brought more rain and more floods. In early summer the earth baked beneath a hot sun. The crops failed and food was scarce.

The people were thin and sad-looking. Nothing grew in the gardens. Nothing grew in the fields. There was no food to be had for love nor money. The animals were just skin and bone. The hot sun had sucked all the goodness from the grass that they ate.

In Dyffryn Conwy, the valley of river Conwy, food was very scarce. That's where Gwion and Siân lived. They were brother and sister. Every day their father walked for miles in search of nuts and wild fruit to eat, but they too were in short supply.

'Ffraid will help us,' said Siân to her brother one day. 'She's a very good woman. She's always helping people.'

'She prays a lot,' said Gwion. 'Perhaps she

will pray for us.'

Ffraid lived in a little round hut with a thatched roof. The hut stood next to the church where she often prayed.

The church had been built by Ffraid and her friends.

'Good morning, children.'

'Good morning, Ffraid. Can you help us find food?' said Siân.

'There's no food in the house,' said Gwion.

'Go home, children,' was Ffraid's reply. 'I shall ask God for food for the people of Dyffryn Conwy.'

In the church Ffraid got down on her knees and prayed for hours on end. As the sun set over the mountains of Snowdonia, the door of the wooden church opened and kind-hearted Ffraid went for a walk along the banks of the Conwy before going to bed.

As she walked, she noticed that the rushes that grew by the river were still green. Everything else had wilted.

As a child in Ireland she had learnt how to make a little sailing boat from one single rush. She made one now and placed it on the water.

She expected the boat to float down towards the sea. Instead it floated upstream against the current. Then she noticed that the boat was coming apart and was swimming like a fish. It was a fish!

Ffraid tossed another rush into the stream - and another - and the same thing happened each time. It was a miracle.

Ffraid ran to Gwion and Siân's house to tell them the good news.   If they threw a handful of rushes into the river, they would have plenty of fish. The fish would keep the people of Dyffryn Conwy alive till the crops grew.

The news spread like wildfire through the valley. Soon a happy band of people had gathered on the river bank. They all had smiles on their faces. The famine was over, thanks to Ffraid.

This happened a long long time ago, but Ffraid's church is still standing. Its name is Llansanffraid. And the strange fish? Yes, they're still in the Conwy river. The local people call them 'brwyniaid' or *rush fish* because they still have the shape and colour of the rushes that Ffraid tossed into the river.

Pale Seiriol and Tanned Cybi

Cybi and Seiriol were two saints. They were great friends. They both wanted to live in a quiet lonely place. So they both went to live on islands off the coast of Ynys Môn, *the isle of Anglesey.*

Cybi lived on Cybi Island and Seiriol lived on Seiriol Island. The sun set over Cybi Island every evening. The sun rose over Seiriol Island every morning.

The two islands are thirty miles apart, so the two saints saw very little of each other. One day they happened to meet.

'Cybi, old friend! It's good to see you again.'

'And you too, Seiriol. How are things with you?'

'Very well, thank you.'

'We must meet more often,' said Cybi.

'Yes, we must,' said Seiriol, 'otherwise we'll lose touch.'

'I know what we'll do,' said Cybi. 'We'll meet in the middle of Anglesey.'

'Where's that?' asked Seiriol.

'It's a place called Clorach. If we meet there, we'll both have exactly the same distance to walk.'

'That's a very good idea,' said Seiriol. 'From now on we'll meet at Clorach.'

The two friends had a long way to walk, so they always set off for Clorach early in the morning. On his way to Clorach Cybi walked in the direction of the rising sun. In the afternoon as he made his way home to Cybi Island, the rays of the setting sun shone on his face. So Cybi's face was always towards the sun and he was nicknamed Tanned Cybi.

For Seiriol it was the other way around. His back was always to the sun when he walked to Clorach from Seiriol Island. On the way home the sun warmed his shoulders. His face was always in shadow and he never caught the sun. So his nickname was Pale Seiriol.

There were two wells in Clorach. The two saints liked to drink the water after their long and thirsty walk. Sometimes another saint called Eilian joined them. The three of them would chat together for hours.

The people of Anglesey began to go to Clorach to be healed, because they knew the saints met there. For them Clorach became a holy place.

One day a mother brought her child to the saints.

'Cybi, Seiriol, please will you cure my little son?' she asked.

'What's wrong?' asked Cybi.

'He was born blind,' said the mother.

'Look, Cybi,' said Seiriol. 'The poor little mite can't open his eyes.'

'Please try and cure him,' begged the mother. 'I have walked many miles to see you today.'

Seiriol cupped his hands and scooped up water from the nearest well. He poured it gently over the baby's eyes so as not to frighten him. Then the saint fell on his knees and prayed to God for help. After saying 'Amen' he got to his feet. As he did so, he heard the baby say 'Mam' in a clear voice. The little boy had opened his eyes and had seen his mother for the very first time.

This was one of many miracles. Seiriol and Cybi lived to a ripe old age. They did many good works and continued to meet for the rest of their lives at the wells at Clorach.

The wells in Clorach dried up long ago. But
people still remember Pale Seiriol and Tanned
Cybi. An important town was named after
Cybi. This is Caergybi, or Holyhead. If you go
to Holyhead, you will see a great church
there. This is the church of Saint Cybi.

On Seiriol Island there are the remains of the
monastery that Seiriol founded. On the
mainland near Penmon there are more

remains. There is also a church that is dedicated to Seiriol.

Beside the church there is a well. Its name is Saint Seiriol's Well. Near the well there are the remains of a little round house made of stone. Seiriol lived in this house before he crossed to Seiriol Island. The house is over one thousand four hundred years old.

The Prince's Ears

There was once a rich prince called March. He was King Arthur's cousin. He lived in Castellmarch, which stood in a beautiful spot near the sea in Pen Llŷn. But, although he was rich and lived in great comfort, March was unhappy. He was unhappy because he had two long hairy ears like horse's ears! In Welsh 'march' means 'horse'. His father had named him March for that very reason.

March kept his hair long to hide his ears. Only one person knew his secret. That person was the barber who sometimes trimmed the ends of his hair. March had warned him to keep the secret on pain of death.

The secret worried the barber greatly. In the end he fell ill and had to go to the doctor.

'Oh, doctor, you must give me some medicine. I can't eat. I can't sleep. I can't do anything!'

'Steady on now. What's troubling you? A headache? A stomach ache?'

'I'm worried, doctor. I'm worried sick.'

'Worried about what?'

'That's the trouble. I can't tell you. I can't tell anyone and that's what's killing me.'

'But you must tell someone or something.'

'Something, doctor? Did you say something?'

'Yes...'

'Oh, thank you! You've just given me a brilliant idea. Goodbye!'

The barber couldn't speak to a person, but he could speak to a thing. He went down to the river Soch and hid in the reeds that grew on its bank. When no one could see him nor hear him, he whispered his secret to the earth. He felt better at once. He had shared his secret and no one was any the wiser...

* * *

Some months later March decided to hold a feast. All the most important people were invited. The finest food was prepared for them. The prince ordered the best bards and musicians to come and entertain his guests.

One of the musicians was a young piper
called Deio Bach. He knew that this was a
very important occasion. He knew too that his
pipe was old and worn.

As he drew near to the castle he had to cross a
river. On its bank he saw some fine long
reeds. They were just what he needed to make
a new pipe. He took out his pocket knife and
began to cut the reeds and whittle away...

That night, after the guests had finished eating, it was the turn of the bards and musicians. Deio Bach was the first on stage. He took a deep breath and began to blow his new pipe. But instead of sweet music, this is what the people heard:

'March has horse's ears! March has horse's ears!'

The prince was absolutely furious. Now everyone knew his secret.

'Take the piper out! Cut off his head at once!'

'But March, it's not my fault,' said Deio Bach. 'I meant to play music. This is a brand new pipe. I made it this afternoon on the river bank. There must be a spell on it. You try playing it.'

The prince blew. Again the people heard:

'March has horse's ears! March has horse's ears!'

Then the barber came forward and said it was his fault. He told March that he had whispered the secret to the river bank. He was sure March would kill him. But instead the prince smiled.

'I thought everyone would laugh at my ears.

That's why I hid them. I have been very foolish.'

From that day on March was happy. He no longer had a secret to hide.

The Devil's Bridge

Once upon a time an old woman lived on the banks of river Mynach. Her name was Mari. Mari had a cow called Modlen who was the apple of her eye. Mari thought the world of her.

Now Modlen liked to wander, but Mari knew she would never go far. She always came home at milking time.

One day Modlen had wandered over the bridge that crossed river Mynach. She had gone to find fresh grass to eat. It was pouring with rain, so the cow sheltered beneath a tree on the far side of the river.

When it was milking time, Mari came out to look for her cowand called as usual: 'Modlen! Modlen! Where are you, bach? Come to Mari, there's a good little cow.'

But Modlen stayed beneath the tree. Mari came to the bridge.

'Oh goodness me, the river has risen! It has almost reached the bridge. Modlen! Modlen! Oh, there you are beneath the tree. Come to Mari.'

Modlen began to cross the bridge, but at once there was a loud noise. The bridge was about to be swept away by the rising river.

'Stay there, Modlen fach! The bridge is breaking!' shouted Mari above the noise of the flood.

At that very moment, with a huge rumble, the bridge broke in pieces. But where was Modlen? Was she still alive? Yes. She was safe, thank goodness. The little cow was standing on a ledge above the river.

'What shall I do now?' wept Mari. 'I can't cross the river. If the water keeps on rising, poor Modlen will drown. Oh, dear me.'

There was another rumble even louder than before. It was a clap of thunder. The first clap was followed by a second, then a third. Mari was so scared, she wrapped her apron round her head. When at last she peeped out, there was a stranger standing by her side.

He looked like a gentleman. On his head he wore a black silk hat. In fact all his clothes were as black as night. He wore a black shirt, a black suit and a black cloak. When Mari looked at his feet, she expected to see black shoes...but instead she saw the hoofs of a goat! The man beside her was

the Devil himself.

Mari pretended not to know him.

'Good evening, Mari,' said the Devil.

'Good evening, sir,' said Mari.

'Why are you crying? Is anything wrong?'

'Yes, sir,' said Mari. 'Modlen is on the other side of the river. The bridge is in pieces. How can I rescue my poor cow?'

'No problem,' said the Devil. 'I'll build you another bridge in the blink of an eye.'

'Will you really, sir?' said Mari innocently. Of course she knew the Devil could do such tricks. She knew too that she must be careful not to be caught by him.

'I will on one condition, Mari,' said the Devil with a sly smile. 'I must be given the first living creature that crosses the bridge.'

'All right, sir,' said Mari.

At that moment there was another clap of thunder and Mari closed her eyes tight. When she opened them again, there was a fine new bridge over river Mynach.

'Would you like to cross the bridge to Modlen?' asked the Devil more slyly than ever. But Mari was not a fool.

'You built that bridge very quickly,' she said. 'Is it safe?'

'Of course it's safe.'

'Well, just to make sure, I'll roll a loaf across the bridge,' said Mari. 'If the bridge can bear the weight of the loaf, I shall then walk across it.'

Mari went to fetch a loaf from the house and rolled it over the bridge. At once a little dog appeared and chased the loaf.

'There you are,' said the Devil. 'The bridge is strong enough.'

'Yes,' said Mari, 'and the first living creature has crossed it. So I'll keep the bridge and you can keep the dog, Mr Devil!'

The Devil was furious and disappeared in a ball of fire. Mari had been too clever for him and soon Modlen was back in her cosy cowshed.

* * *

The bridge still crosses river Mynach at the village called Devil's Bridge. Today there are three bridges, one on top of the other, and people come from all over the world to see them.

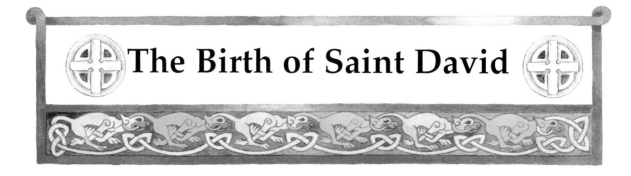

The Birth of Saint David

Many countries have a saint who watches over them. This special saint is called a patron saint. The patron saint of Wales is Saint David - *Dewi Sant*. Because he was such an important man, many tales are told about him. One tale tells of his birth in Pembrokeshire.

David's father was called Sandde. He was the son of Prince Ceredig. Ceredig was prince of Ceredigion and gave his name to that part of Wales.

David's mother was called Non. She was the daughter of Cynir, an important man who lived in Pembrokeshire.

Sadly there were evil people who hated Non and Sandde. Non knew it was important to find a special place where her baby could be born in safety. Non chose a lovely spot overlooking the sea. She hid there from her enemies.

At the time of David's birth there was a terrible storm. Flashes of lightning lit up the night sky. Thunder made the earth tremble. Huge hailstones knocked the leaves off the trees. The storm was so fierce that David's enemies had to flee for their lives.

The name of the place where David was born is Capel Non, or Saint Non's Chapel. Though the storm raged over the whole of Pembrokeshire, in Capel Non all was quiet. When our patron saint was born, a strange light, brighter than the

sun, shone on the place. At the very same moment a well sprang up close by. Non drank the water and that is why it was called Saint Non's Well.

Later David was baptised. A blind monk was present. The priest got ready to pour water onto David's forehead.

'I christen you David,' he said.

As he spoke, some of the water splashed onto the blind man. At once there came a shout:

'I can see! I can see!'

Everyone fell on their knees. Though David was only a tiny baby, he had performed a miracle. During the course of his long life he performed many more.

During his life David wandered far and wide. He built churches in many of the places where he lived. In Llanddewibrefi there is a famous church that bears David's name. But David's main home was the church which he built in Glyn Rhosyn. It stood about a mile from Capel Non where he was born. He spent most of his life there. That is why the place is still called St David's.

You remember the story of the blind monk who regained his sight when David's christening water fell on him? Strangely enough the water of Saint Non's Well is also good for the eyes. This was the well that sprang from the earth on the night that David was born. People from far and near still visit the well. They bathe their sore eyes in the water and hope for a cure.

People from all over the world still visit St David's too. If you ever visit this beautiful part of Wales, remember to go to Capel Non and see the very place where Wales's patron saint was born.

Arthur's Cave

One of Wales's greatest heroes is King Arthur. I'm sure you know the story of his last battle against his enemy, Medrod. Arthur was wounded and was taken away to be healed. Some say he went to the Isle of Avalon. Others say he went to a cave in Snowdonia. Many claim that Arthur's Cave is in southern Wales and this is the story they tell.

Siôn was a drover. He would walk to the great fairs of England, taking with him cattle, sheep and even geese to sell. The biggest fair was in the biggest city, which was London. There were two things which a good drover needed - a faithful dog and a stout stick.

Siôn was going to London for the very first time, so he decided to make himself a new stick. Near Pont Nedd Fechan he saw a hazel tree. He cut off one of its branches and began to make himself a stick. He would finish the stick long before he got to London.

Siôn and the other drovers walked for days. Siôn whittled away at the stick as he walked. At last they could see London in the distance. As Siôn was walking with his friends over London Bridge a stranger came up to him.

'Good afternoon,' said the stranger.

'Good afternoon,' said Siôn.

'Where have you come from?'

'From Carmarthenshire,' said Siôn.

'Have you indeed? And was that where you found the stick?'

'No. I found it in Pont Nedd Fechan. Why are you asking?'

'For no particular reason,' said the stranger. 'Could you show me the very tree where you found the stick?'

'I suppose so.'

'Right. I'll walk back to Wales with you after you have sold your animals.'

And that's what happened. Siôn was puzzled by the man. He was sure he had a secret. In the end the man confessed he was a wizard. For years he had been searching for the very tree from which the stick was made. He had to find the tree because there was treasure buried beneath it.

After many days of hard walking Siôn and the wizard arrived in Pont Nedd Fechan.

'That's the tree!' said Siôn excitedly.

'Good,' said the wizard. 'There is a cave beneath the tree. The treasure is in the cave, but we must be careful.'

'Why?' asked Siôn.

'It is King Arthur's treasure. Arthur is sleeping in the cave with his army. We must be careful not to wake him.'

At once the wizard began to dig. Soon he uncovered a flat stone. When they lifted the stone, Sion saw steps leading down into the earth. They had found Arthur's Cave!

The two crept down into the cave with a lamp each. At the far end Siôn saw a huge heap of gold and silver. He was about to rush towards it, when the wizard stopped him. He pointed to a bell hanging nearby and told Siôn that this was the bell that would wake Arthur and his army. If the bell rang, Arthur would ask:

'Has the day come?'

Then they would have to reply:
'No. Sleep on.'

It was very important to remember those exact words. If they did, they could take the treasure from the cave.

By this time Siôn's eyes had got used to the darkness. He saw thousands of soldiers

sleeping in the cave. A man wearing a golden crown slept beside the treasure. It was King Arthur himself!

Siôn and the wizard filled their sacks with gold. They carried the treasure out safely and the wizard went away.

Siôn wanted more treasure. He went back into

the cave and this time he brushed against the bell. At once Arthur woke up, but the drover remembered the words. The king went back to sleep.

The same happened the next time he went into the cave. Once again Arthur went back to sleep.

By now there was a huge heap of gold at the foot of the tree. But it wasn't enough for Siôn.

He decided to fetch another sackful. This time, in his haste, he forgot the words. Arthur's soldiers woke up and saw him stealing the treasure.

The greedy drover was given a good hiding by Arthur's soldiers. Then he was thrown out of the cave. When he recovered, there was no sign of the treasure. Siôn spent the rest of his life searching for the tree and the cave beneath it. He never found them again.

Teilo's Skull

Teilo was a saint who lived at the same time as Saint David. The two of them were born in Pembrokeshire. They also went to the same school. Teilo built his first church in Pembrokeshire. This was the church of Llandeilo near Maenclochog.

Later on Teilo built churches across South Wales. The most important of these was the church on the banks of the Taff at Llandaff. By today Llandaff is part of Cardiff, but the cathedral church still stands there. Near the cathedral there is a small well. Its name is Saint Teilo's Well.

One day one of Teilo's friends came to him.

'Teilo! Teilo! I have bad news for you.'

'What's happened?'

'A terrible illness has reached Wales. They call it the Yellow Plague. It has already killed thousands of people in the north.'

'Why is that?' said Teilo.

'They say that the illness is like a huge yellow monster that stalks the land. They say that anyone who sees the monster dies. They say that Maelgwn, prince of Gwynedd, hid in a church from the monster.'

'Was he safe in the church?' asked Teilo.

'No. He looked through the keyhole and saw the yellow monster.'

'What happened to him?'

'He fell down dead on the spot.'

When Teilo heard this, he decided to leave Wales for a while. The saint and his followers went to stay in Brittany till the Yellow Plague had gone. Teilo did not sail to Brittany in a boat. Instead he rode on the back of a magic horse which could gallop over the waves. Teilo lived in Brittany for seven years.

After that he lived in St David's for a while. Then he moved to live near Llandaff, his favourite church. After a long life which was spent doing good works, Teilo died. But that is not the end of the story, not by a long way...

Shortly before he died, Teilo called his maid.

'After I have died, they are going to bury my body at Llandeilo on the banks of the Tywi. One year after my death I want you to take my skull to the first church that I built. Will you do that for me?'

'I will, master.'

'I'm glad to hear it. It's very important.'

And that was what happened. A year after his death Teilo's skull was moved to the church he built near Maenclochog in Pembrokeshire.

He had made a well there. Its name, of course, was Saint Teilo's Well. Sick people came to the well from far and near to look for a cure. The best hope of a cure was to use the saint's skull

as a cup and drink from it. Those who did not drink from the skull were not cured.

The people living in the farmhouse near the well looked after the skull. For hundreds of years they lent the skull to anyone who wanted to drink the water. About seventy years ago one member of the family sold the skull. No one knew who had bought it. Nothing was heard of it for many years.

Then a few years ago the saint's skull was found. So the story has a happy ending. The skull was given to Llandaff Cathedral, Teilo's favourite church, and there it remains.

There are many places called Llandeilo in Wales. Today 'llan' means church, but in Teilo's time it meant a piece of land marked out for a saint's use. Perhaps the most famous Llandeilo is the town of Llandeilo in Carmarthenshire. This town grew around the church of Teilo and is known as Llandeilo Fawr.

At least a dozen churches in South Wales bear Teilo's name. One of them actually moved fourteen miles to the outskirts of Cardiff not so long ago. This is the church of Llandeilo Tal-y-bont. At one time it used to stand near Pontardulais, but now craftsmen have moved it to the Folk Museum in St Fagan's. Perhaps you'll go there and visit it one day.

The Wicked Giant of Gilfach Fargod

Once upon a time more fairies lived around Gelli-gaer than anywhere else in Glamorgan.

Fairies are tiny, but very beautiful, creatures. They are as happy as larks and the people of the Rhymney Valley loved to hear them dance and sing.

Then one day a huge, ugly, wicked giant built himself a home in Gilfach Fargod. His home was an enormous tower with a garden around it. The giant had long matted hair and a big straggly beard. His clothes were scruffy and dirty and wherever he went he carried a stout stick in his hand. Twisted around the stick was a long, long snake.

The giant hated all his neighbours. Instead of 'Welcome' on his doormat, he had the words, 'Go away'. The only person he liked was a huge witch, who was as ugly as himself. She was his girlfriend.

The giant hated the fairies especially. Soon the fairies were too scared to dance by moonlight. On moonlit nights the giant came looking for them along the Rhymney Valley with his stick

in his hand. The ground trembled beneath his huge boots and the little dancers stayed indoors in case they were trampled by him. Soon the fairy circles disappeared and their sweet songs were no longer heard in the valley.

One day one of the fairies went to the court of Queen Belene and asked if he could speak to her.

'What do you want, Gwarwyn?' the queen asked kindly.

'I'd like your permission to kill the giant,' the boy replied.

'But you know that is against our rules.'

'I know that,' said Gwarwyn, 'but the giant has killed my parents. We must stop him before he kills us all.'

'That's true,' said Belene, 'but be careful, Gwarwyn.'

The following night Gwarwyn crept out of his hiding-place and went to the forest of Pencoed Fawr near Bedwellty. He knew that an owl lived in an oak tree in the middle of the woods. The owl is the wisest of birds. Gwarwyn could speak the language of the birds, so he went to the wise bird and asked how he could kill the giant.

'The giant sleeps by day,' said the owl. 'That is when the fairies must bend a branch of the

apple tree that grows outside his garden and make a huge bow. Then you must place a huge arrow in the bow. That's all you need to do. I'll do the rest.'

Gwarwyn tried to get the fairies to go to the giant's house, but at first no one was willing. They could hear him snore, but they were afraid to go near.

'What if he wakes up?'

'He won't, if we're quiet,' said Gwarwyn. 'We can't live in fear for ever. Who is brave enough to come with me?'

At last one of the fairies raised his hand. Then another, and another...

That afternoon the bow was made and the arrow put in place while the giant snored.

The giant often used to meet his girlfriend, the ugly witch, beneath the apple tree. That night the witch was late. As the owl floated silently past the giant's house, she saw him beneath the tree. She landed gently on the highest branch and loosed the arrow. The giant was killed on the spot. The huge snake on his stick also died. As quick as a flash the owl placed another arrow in the bow and, when the witch arrived, she was shot cold dead.

The giant, the witch and the snake were buried beneath the tree. The fairies of Gelli-gaer were happy once more. On moonlit nights, the sounds of their singing and

dancing echoed throughout the valley and their fairy circles were seen all around...

But two strange things happened after the death of the wicked giant, the ugly witch and the big snake. Before she died, the witch said that only sour little apples would grow outside garden walls. And that is true even today.

And the second strange thing? Well, on the snake's grave pretty red flowers grew. They too are still with us today and are called 'Snake Flowers', even though this happened a long time ago in Wales.

Additional notes and activities

THE CHARACTERS FROM THE STORIES

Arthur:
Arthur is a historical character. He was a military leader who lived around the end of the fifth century. Because of his many victories over the Saxons, he became a legendary figure. When he died, there was a tradition that he was only sleeping and would one day return to lead the Welsh to freedom. Later folk tales honoured him with the title of king and he plays an important role in the tale of Culhwch and Olwen. The story of Arthur spread throughout Europe and other tales grew around him, such as *Y Tair Rhamant* (lit. The Three Romances) in which he is a mighty king to whom the Knights of the Round Table owe allegiance. In some tales Arthur goes to the Isle of Avalon after he is wounded by the traitor Medrod. In others, such as the tale here recorded, he retreats to a cave with his faithful soldiers. Throughout Wales there are many caves known as Arthur's Cave.

Belene:
One of the traditional names of the Tylwyth Teg *(the Fairies)*.

Brochwel:
Prince of Powys in the sixth century. He was nicknamed Brochwel Ysgithrog (Brochwel of the Tusks) because of his tusks or long teeth. His chief court was situated in Pengwern near Shrewsbury. Tradition has it that he gave the land around Pennant Melangell to Saint Melangell after failing to kill a hare and after he had recognised the piety of the princess who had fled from Ireland.

Cybi:
A sixth-century saint who founded many churches throughout Wales. His chief settlement was the monastery which he built on the site of an old Roman fort at Holyhead (Caergybi). According to tradition he was nicknamed Tanned Cybi and was a close friend of Saint Seiriol, or Pale Seiriol.

Ffraid:
A sixth-century Irish saint who founded many churches in Wales and the Celtic countries. In Ireland, where she is known as Brigid, she is considered one of the country's most important saints. A rush cross known as 'Brigid's Cross' can still be seen in many an Irish home. She is said to have sailed to Wales on a turf sod that broke free of the Irish mainland and landed in the Conwy estuary. Later she saved the people of Dyffryn Conwy from famine when she created the 'rush fish' that are still seen in the river. The church of Llansanffraid stands on the banks of river Conwy at Glan Conwy.

Gwarwyn:
A traditional fairy name. It is found in oral folk tales. One variation of the name is Gwarwyn-a-throt.

Maelgwn:
Maelgwn Gwynedd, a historical character who was prince of Gwynedd and who died of the Yellow Plague around the year 547. His chief court was at Deganwy, not far from the river Conwy. He was a powerful prince and a descendant of Cunedda Wledig. According to tradition he took refuge from the Yellow Plague in the church of Rhos, near Deganwy, but died after peeping through the keyhole and seeing the plague in the form of a hideous yellow monster.

March:
A legendary character. His full name is March Amheirchion or March ap Meirchion. He features in a number of tales and traditions. In the most well-known of these tales he is associated with Castellmarch, near Abersoch, Llŷn.

Melangell:
Melangell was an Irish princess who fled to Wales to avoid marrying a man whom she did not love. She is traditionally considered to be the patron saint of the animals of Wales after she rescued a hare from the hunt led by Brochwel Ysgithrog. She founded a nunnery in Pennant Melangell, where the church named after her still stands. In the church there is a fine shrine to the saint.

Non:
The mother of Saint David. She was the

daughter of Cynir, a prince of Pembrokeshire and her mother Anna was, according to one tradition, the sister of King Arthur. The ruins of Capel Non - St Non's Chapel - where David was born, and St Non's Well which sprang up at that time, are to be found about a mile from St David's. Many churches and villages are named after her.

Sandde:
The father of Saint David. He was the son of Ceredig, the king who gave his name to Ceredigion.

Seiriol:
A sixth-century saint who came from the line of the royal family of Gwynedd and lived at the same time as Maelgwn Gwynedd. He founded the church of Penmaenmawr and Penmon Abbey. According to tradition he was nicknamed Pale Seiriol and was a close friend of Saint Cybi, or Tanned Cybi.

Tegid Foel:
A fictional character. He appears in this folk tale and also in 'Hanes Taliesin', the story of the strange birth of the bard Taliesin. In that story he lives in Bala with his wife Ceridwen and his son Afagddu. According to tradition Llyn Tegid (Bala Lake) was named after Tegid Foel and his vanished town, the first town of Bala.

Teilo:
A sixth-century saint. His story can be found in The Life of Teilo, written in the twelfth century. He was born at Penalun (Penally), Pembrokeshire and is said to have been a friend of Saint David. According to tradition Teilo, David and Padarn went on a pilgrimage to Jerusalem. After he returned to Wales he had to flee to Brittany for seven years and seven months because of the deadly plague known as The Yellow Plague. After that he was busy setting up churches throughout South Wales. The most important of these were Llandeilo, Carmarthenshire and Llandaff Cathedral, near Cardiff. His skull is now kept at the cathedral after having been lost for some years.

A BRIEF GLOSSARY

The Secret of Bala Lake
gwyniad - a whitefish, found especially in Bala Lake

The Rush Fish of the River Conwy
Ffraid - Brigid, Bride
rush fish - sparling, smelt

Pale Seiriol and Tanned Cybi
Cybi Island - Holy Island
Seiriol Island - Puffin Island

The Prince's Ears
bard - poet
Pen Llŷn - the Llŷn Peninsula

The Wicked Giant of Gilfach Fargod
sour little apples - crab apples
snake flowers - red campion

ACTIVITIES

Melangell

Written:

1. Compose a simple poem about the life of the saint. (The group Plethyn sings a song in Welsh about Melangell.)
2. Write an imaginative description of a day in the life of a wild animal or of a pet.
3. Write a factual piece describing what should and should not be done when keeping an animal of any kind, whether its a pet or a farm animal.

Oral:

1. Encourage the children to read other stories about animals and to tell those stories to the class. e.g. the story of Gelert; the story of Saint Francis; Noah's Ark; Aesop's fables.
2. Name the animals that live in the locality. Where do they live? e.g. fox - den; snail - shell.
3. Discuss, sing and learn nursery rhymes, such as Ding Dong Bell, Baby Bunting, Bonheddwr Mawr o'r Bala.
4. Ask the children to tell the story of Melangell from the point of view of Brochwel, Melangell and the hare.

The Secret of Bala Lake

Written:

1. The diary of Dafydd the harpist in the days before and after the drowning of the old town of Bala.
2. The story involves a vanished town. In all localities there are traces of ancient settlements - a Stone Age cave, maybe, or a Celtic fort or a Roman town. The children could visit the site and then describe what it would be like to live in such a place.
3. Tegi is mentioned at the end of the story. Tegi is a creature similar to the Loch Ness monster. Ask the children to try and imagine what Tegi would look like and then to write a brief description. They could also draw a picture.

Oral:

1. This is one of many tales involving lost lands or cities. In Wales we have a number of such tales - Cantre'r Gwaelod, Tyno Helyg, the lost town of Llyn Safaddan (*Llangorse Lake*) and many others. These tales could be told to the class along with other tales such as Ker Iz (off the coast of Brittany) and Atlantis. The tales may then be discussed and compared.
2. Revenge plays an important part in the story. But is revenge good or bad? This can be discussed in relation to the children's own experiences on the school yard, or with brothers and sisters and so on.
3. Tegid lost a whole town. Have the children ever lost anything precious? How? How did they feel?

The Rush Fish of River Conwy

Written:

1. Collect names and pictures of fish that live in local rivers and lakes.
2. Compose a prayer asking for help for those in need such as the poor and needy of the Third World.
3. Write a letter to be included in a shoe box organised by Operation Christmas Child.

Oral:

1. Discuss the weather and its importance. Collect and discuss weather sayings, such as various descriptions of rain, weather signs and so on.
2. Discuss the dangers of a prolonged spell of weather - rain, sun, snow or wind - as happens in the story. The children can pretend to be weather forecasters commenting on extreme weather conditions.
3. Introduce the idea of famine, which often results from too much sun or drought in the Third World.

Pale Seiriol and Tanned Cybi

Written:

1. The points of the compass are an important element of this story. A map of the area where the story takes place could lead to practical compass work: finding the North, showing that the sun rises in the East and sets in the West, and so on.
2. The two saints had nicknames. The children could investigate the stories behind certain nicknames, such as the Cuckoos of Dolwyddelan, Swansea Jacks, Pembrokeshire Pigs, and so on.
3. Walking and travelling are an important theme. Ask the children to write a description of their own journey to school.

Oral:

1. What is the children's favourite walk? Discuss and investigate the importance of the senses; what can they see, hear, smell, and so on?

2. Give instructions orally on how to reach a certain place or building.

3. Collect all kinds of nicknames. Have a fun session during which the children invent new nicknames. Introduce the idea of alliteration.

The Prince's Ears

Written:

1. A harpist is mentioned in the story. This could lead to written work on different occupations or the class could concentrate on one single occupation and invite a practitioner (a doctor, nurse, a vet or a bus driver, for example) to the school to discuss his/her work with the children beforehand.

2. The harp is one of the national symbols of Wales, but it is only one of many musical instruments. Compile a table/graph dividing the instruments into groups - string, wind, percussion and so on.

3. Design a poster or letter inviting guests to Prince March's feast.

Oral:

1. The essence of the story is the burden placed on an individual who has to keep a secret. Discuss this in class and demonstrate the importance of sharing a secret.

2. Dramatise and act scenes from the story.

3. Is there an old building in your locality with a story attached to it? The children could interview local people and then report to the class.

The Devil's Bridge

Written:

1. Complete a story that starts with the words: 'One day as I crossed the bridge....'

2. Write the autobiography of a bridge.

3. A cow called Modlen is mentioned in the story. Collect traditional names of cows, dogs or other animals. Compile a list of the children's pets and their names.

Oral:

1. Ask the children to collect stories about bridges in the area and to tell them to the class.

2. Discuss various uses of the word 'bridge,' e.g. bridge of the nose, a violin bridge, to bridge a gap.

3. Look at a map of Wales and see how many place names contain the word 'bridge' or 'pont'.

4. Discuss different ways of crossing water: a ford, stepping stones, bridges (of various kinds), a ferry and so on.

The Birth of Saint David

Written:

1. Ask the children to pretend that they are the blind monk whose eyesight was restored at David's christening and then to write a letter to their family describing what happened, what was the first thing they saw, and so on.

2. Compile a Wordsearch for the class containing names and words from the story.

3. Name the patron saints of other countries. Are there stories about them?

4. Because the weather plays such an important role in the story, the children could be asked to write descriptive pieces, such as: a storm at sea; a hot summer's day; the autumn wind.

Oral:

1. Ask the children to talk about a place that is special to them. They can describe the place and explain why it is so important to them.

2. Invite one of the children to pretend that he/she is Saint David/Non and then to answer questions from the class based on the story.

3. Ask the children to find out if there are any healing wells in the area and then to report to the rest of the class. This lesson could be taped.

4. The class could discuss the effects of infirmity with reference to the blind man in the story e.g. make a list of the things they'd miss seeing if they were blind.

Arthur's Cave

Written:

1. A particular tree features in this story. The children could collect names of trees in the locality and then learn how to recognise them. This could lead to nature table work with leaves and fruit.

2. Gold and silver are not the only treasure. Encourage the children to write about their most precious possesssion.

3. Write a story about hidden treasure.

Oral:

1. In the story the drover was on his way to a fair in London. Years ago many fairs were held in Wales. Ask the children to collect old pictures and discuss them in class.
2. A light-hearted session discussing where the children would hide treasure, if the need arose.
3. Get the children to describe the wizard's feelings when he saw the drover with the stick in his hand on London Bridge; the drover's feelings when he ventured into the cave for the first time; Arthur's feelings when he was woken for no good reason.
4. This is essentially a story about greed. Ask the children to write a short play that contains a moral.

Teilo's Skull

Written:

1. Many different towns called Llandeilo are mentioned in the story. Make a collection of local place names beginning with 'Llan' and see how many are called after a saint. Note any story or legend associated with them.
2. Continue a story beginning with the words: 'A long time ago...'
3. Healing is the main theme of this story. The children could write about their experience of illness and how they got well again.

Oral:

1. Though the well in the story is a healing well, the chief function of a well was to provide a supply of water. How do people get water today? Where does it come from? How?
2. Discuss why there was more illness and disease in times gone by.
3. Llandeilo Tal-y-bont was moved to the Folk Museum in St Fagan's. Why was that? Is there any building in the locality which the children would like to preserve by moving it to St Fagan's?

The Wicked Giant of Gilfach Fargod

Written:

1. A particular wild flower is named in the story. Compile a list of the names of local wild flowers, including regional names.
2. Happiness and sadness form part of the story. Ask the children to compose a list of comparisons: - as happy as...; - as sad as....
3. Belene talks of rules. Ask the children to draw up or collect a list of rules such as school rules, the rules of the countryside, crossing the road and so on.

Oral:

1. In the story Gwarwyn talks to an owl. The children could compose an impromptu dialogue between themselves and another kind of bird such as a robin, a cuckoo, a seagull, a swan.
2. In the written work the children composed a list of comparisons: as happy as..., as sad as.... This could be taken a step further by discussing what makes a person sad and what makes a person happy.
3. Discuss the importance of rules and why they are drawn up. Invite people to school (a policeman or a countryside warden for instance) to discuss their work with the children and to answer questions.

Llyfrau darllen difyr, llawn lluniau lliwgar yn seiliedig ar straeon gwerin Cymru

STRAEON CYMRU

Mae'r gyfres hon yn llenwi bwlch wrth gyflwyno rhai o straeon gorau ein gwlad i'r to sy'n codi. Lluniau lliw trawiadol gan Carys Owen. 36 tud. yr un.

1. GELERT

Mae hanes Gelert, ci ffyddlon y tywysog Llywelyn, yn un sydd wedi cyrraedd calonnau plant Cymru ers cenedlaethau. Dyma hi'n cael ei hadrodd o'r newydd ar gyfer ton arall o blant sydd bob amser yn mwynhau stori dda.
Elena Morus, Rhif Rhyngwladol: 0-86381-291-0, £3.25

2. OLWEN

Dyma un o chwedlau hynaf yr iaith Gymraeg. Stori liwgar, llawn rhamant ac antur am y modd y llwyddodd arwr ifanc o'r enw Culhwch i ennill Olwen, merch y cawr, yn wraig.
Elena Morus, Rhif Rhyngwladol: 0-86381-292-9, £3.50

3. CLUSTIAU MARCH

Chwedl sy'n adrodd hanes am y Brenin March ap Meirchion a'i glustiau anhygoel, ac am y modd y daeth y bobl i wybod am gyfrinach ei glustiau.
Elena Morus, Rhif Rhyngwladol: 0-86381-329-1, £3.50

4. CANTRE'R GWAELOD

Hanes boddi Cantre'r Gwaelod yw un o chwedlau mwyaf adnabyddus Cymru. Hanes y môr creulon yn torri'r mur uchel oedd yn amddiffyn y wlad oherwydd esgeulustod y pen-gwyliwr, Seithenyn.
Elena Morus, Rhif Rhyngwladol: 0-86381-363-1, £3.50

5. MERCH Y LLYN

Dyma un o chwedlau gwerin mwyaf adnabyddus Cymru. Hanes llawn rhamant a thristwch am y gŵr ifanc o'r Mynydd Du a syrthiodd mewn cariad dros ei ben a'i glustiau â'r ferch arallfydol o Lyn y Fan Fach.
Esyllt Nest Roberts, Rhif Rhyngwladol: 0-86381-414-X, £3.50

6. DINAS EMRYS

Dyma hanes y brenin Gwrtheyrn a geisiodd godi castell ar fryn wrth droed yr Wyddfa flynyddoedd maith yn ôl. Ond roedd rhywun, neu rywbeth, yn benderfynol o'i atal.
Esyllt Nest Roberts, Rhif Rhyngwladol: 0-86381-439-5, £3.50

7. DWYNWEN

Ionawr y 25ain yw'r diwrnod pan fydd cariadon yn gyrru cardiau ac anrhegion i'w gilydd i ddathlu dydd gŵyl Santes Dwynwen. Ond pwy oedd Dwynwen a pham ydan ni'n cofio amdani fel hyn?

Esyllt Nest Roberts, Rhif Rhyngwladol: 0-86381-468-9, £3.50

8. ELIDIR A'R TYLWYTH TEG

Wrth guddio ar lan afon Nedd daw Elidir o hyd i dwnnel i wlad y Tylwyth Teg. Daw'n gyfeillgar iawn â'r bobl bach ond mae'r chwarae'n troi'n chwerw . . .

Esyllt Nest Roberts, Rhif Rhyngwladol: 0-86381-530-8, £3.50

9. BLODEUWEDD

Stori'r ferch o flodau.

Esyllt Nest Roberts, Rhif Rhyngwladol: 0-86381-569-3, £3.50

CADOG A'R LLYGODEN

Roedd newyn mawr yn y tir – y tywydd yn sych, dim yn tyfu a'r bobl yn llwglyd ac yn wan o ddiffyg bwyd. Mynach oedd yn benderfynol o geisio helpu'r bobl druan oedd Cadog ac mae pethau'n gwella pan gaiff gymorth llygoden fach fywiog . . .

Rhif Rhyngwladol: 0-86381-416-6

RHYS A CHWCW RHISGA

Stori am y gog ydi hon, stori am y dyddiau hapus hynny pan glywn ni'r gog yn canu. Dyddiau'r gwanwyn, dyddiau'r haf ac yn Rhisga, fel mewn llawer lle arall, doedd y bobl ddim eisiau gweld y gog yn eu gadael . . .

Rhif Rhyngwladol: 0-86381-418-2

Dau lyfr clawr caled, maint A4, llawn lluniau lliwgar, 16 tud., £2.99 yr un.

Stori: Siân Lewis
Dylunio: Gini Wade

Argraffiad newydd # Straeon ac Arwyr Gwerin Cymru

12 stori werin gan John Owen Huws wedi'u dylunio gan Catrin Meirion. Cyfnod Allweddol 2.
Y Wibernant; Ifor Bach; Dreigiau Myrddin Emrys; Taliesin; Gwrachod Llanddona; Morwyn Llyn y Fan; Elidir; Caradog; Cae'r Melwr; Dewi Sant; Breuddwyd Macsen; Cantre'r Gwaelod
160 tud; maint A5; Rhif Rhyngwladol: 0-86381-575-8; Pris: £4.75

Ar gael yn eich siopau lleol, neu drwy gysylltu â swyddfa'r wasg:
Gwasg Carreg Gwalch, 12 Iard yr Orsaf, Llanrwst, Dyffryn Conwy, LL26 0EH
01492 642031   01492 641502   llyfrau@carreg.gwalch.co.uk
Lle ar y we: www.carreg-gwalch.co.uk

Colourful and entertaining reading books, based on traditional Welsh tales

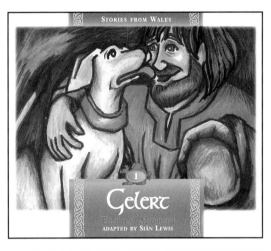

STORIES FROM WALES

This series introduces some of our country's best-loved stories to a new generation, with plenty of eyecatching colour illustrations by Carys Owen.

1. GELERT

The tale of Gelert, Prince Llywelyn's faithful hound, has touched the hearts of Welsh children for generations. Here, it is told anew for another generation of children who enjoy a good story.
Elena Morus; Adapted by Siân Lewis ISBN: 0-86381-392-5, £3.50

2. OLWEN

One of the oldest Welsh legends. A colourful tale of romance and adventure, which tells how a young hero named Culhwch succeeded in winning the hand of Olwen, the giant's daughter, in marriage.
Elena Morus; Adapted by Siân Lewis ISBN: 0-86381-393-3, £3.50

3. THE KING'S EARS

A legend recounting the tale of King March ap Meirchion and his incredible ears, and of how the people found out about his secret.
Elena Morus; Adapted by Siân Lewis ISBN: 0-86381-394-1, £3.50

4. THE LOST LAND

The tale of the drowning of Cantre' Gwaelod which lay on the shores of Cardigan Bay. Seithenyn was the sentry in charge of the sea wall, but Seithenyn was lazy.
Elena Morus; Adapted by Siân Lewis ISBN: 0-86381-524-3, £3.50

5. THE LADY OF THE LAKE

A tale of sadness and romance, which tells how Hywel falls in love with the beautiful and mysterious lady of the lake.
Esyllt Nest Roberts; Adapted by Siân Lewis ISBN: 0-86381-525-1, £3.50

6. DINAS EMRYS

Long, long ago King Gwrtheyrn tried to build a castle at the foot of Snowdon. But however hard he tried, someone – or something was determined to stop him.
Esyllt N Roberts; Adapted by Siân Lewis ISBN: 0-86381-526-X, £3.50

To be published in 1999:

7. DWYNWEN
The patron saint of lovers in Wales.

8. ELIDIR
An adventure with the king of the fairies.

9. THE FLOWER MAIDEN
The story of the maiden that was wizarded from flowers.

£3.50 each

STRAEON CYMRU

DWYNWEN

ESYLLT NEST ROBERTS

FOLK-TALES FROM WALES

CADOG AND THE MOUSE

Story: Siân Lewis
Illustrations: Gini Wade

RHYS AND THE CUCKOO OF RISCA

Story: Siân Lewis
Illustrations: Gini Wade

CADOG AND THE MOUSE
There was a great famine in the land – the season was dry, nothing grew and the people were weak with hunger. But a kind monk, Cadog, decided to help these poor people find food. Things began to look up when he met a little lively mouse . . .
ISBN: 0-86381-417-4

RHYS AND THE CUCKOO OF RISCA
This is a story about the cuckoo, a story about those happy days when we hear the cuckoo's song. Spring days, summer days and at Risca, like many other places, the people did not want to see the cuckoo leaving . . .
ISBN: 0-86381-419-0

Two hard back books, A4 size, full colour illustrations, 16 page, £2.99 each.

**Story: Siân Lewis
Illustrations: Gini Wade**

A Railway Story for Key Stage 2 **The Ffestiniog Adventure**
by Pamela Roberts; illustrations by John Shackell.
A completely new kind of train journey is waiting for four lively children when they are staying with their grandpa. This - a real steam railway - is the Ffestiniog Adventure.
48 pages; A5 size; ISBN: 0-86381-548-0; Price: £2.99

Available at your local bookshops or by contacting the press:
Gwasg Carreg Gwalch, 12 Iard yr Orsaf, Llanrwst, Dyffryn Conwy, LL26 0EH
✆ 01492 642031   🖷 01492 641502   ✆ books@carreg-gwalch.co.uk
Internet: www.carreg-gwalch.co.uk